Dragon and Mousie

First impression: 2002
Welsh edition: 2002
© Copyright: Andrew Fusek Peters, Gini Wade & Y Lolfa Cyf., 2002
Illustrations: Gini Wade

ISBN: 0 86243 650 8

Printed and published in Wales by
Y Lolfa Cyf., Talybont, Ceredigion SY24 5AP
e-mail ylolfa@ylolfa.com
website www.ylolfa.com
phone (01970) 832 304
fax 832 782
isdn 832 813

Dragon and Mousie

Andrew Fusek Peters
illustrations by Gini Wade

Dragon and Mousie lived in a far away forest.
Dragon was green
like the leaves on the tree.
Mousie was brown as a walnut.

Together, they played all day long, Dragon so big
and Mousie so small.
When Dragon laughed, it sounded like thunder.
When Mousie giggled, it sounded like rain.

They played hide and seek with the wind
in the trees, and skipping games
with spiders' webs.
When they grew cold,
Dragon lit a fire with his nose!

For lunch, they drank blackberry juice
and dined on hazelnut pie with acorn soup.

One day, after lunch, Dragon roared:
"I'm bored! Come on, let's go exploring!"
"Yes please!" squeaked Mousie,
"But my little legs are tired!"

So Dragon unfolded his great green wings
and Mousie climbed into his pocket.
She peeped out over the edge
as they soared into the sky.
Soon, they were high above the trees.

They flew for hours over rivers, mountains and strange new forests.
Time flew with them, and the sun
began to get ready for bed.

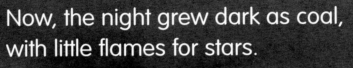

Now, the night grew dark as coal,
with little flames for stars.
"Dragon!" squeaked Mousie in a tiny
voice, "I want to go home!"
But Dragon and Mousie were lost.

Far up in the heavens,
Mrs Moon smiled down
with her big, beaming face.
"Have you lost your way, my dears?"
she tinkled.
"Oh yes!" sighed Dragon.
"Suddenly everywhere looks the same!"
"Don't you worry yourselves,
I have just the thing!" sang Mrs Moon.

13

Then she reached into her handbag and pulled out
a silver ribbon.
She shook it out across the sky
and it turned into a path of moonbeams
with stars to light their way.
"You'll be home in a twinkle," she said.
Dragon and Mousie waved goodbye
and followed the path all the way back.

14

"We're home!" squealed Mousie with delight.
Home was high in an old oak tree.
They climbed up the stairs of their tree house,
up and up, until they could
almost touch the sky.

High in a hollow of the oak
was a steaming silver pool.
It was bathtime under the stars!
The water was deliciously warm.
Goldfish darted around like little lamps.
Mousie jumped into the pool with a splash
and Dragon blew big bubbles.

After their bath, they shivered as they put on pyjamas woven from leaves and spider thread.

A door opened in the trunk of the tree. In the corner of their bedroom, a fire glowed. Under the eaves, a window let in the smile of Mrs Moon.

Grandragon Treetop sat in an armchair by the fire,
ready to read them a bedtime book.
"I was worried. I wondered where you were!" he said.
"We got lost and Mrs Moon showed us the way home,"
squeaked Mousie.
"I am sure she did," said Grandragon
and began to read.

The bedtime book told of creatures
called Boys and Girls.
"They are little animals with two twigs
for arms and two sticks for legs!"
laughed Grandragon.
"They don't really exist, do they?" roared Dragon.
"Who knows?" said Grandragon.
"But I do know it's time for bed!"

He tucked them in, blew out the lamp
and damped the fire down.

Dragon and Mousie snuggled into their warm beds.
Outside, shooting stars played hopscotch in the Milky Way
and the trees whispered spooky stories in the night.

What a wonderful day!
Dragon and Mousie drifted off to sleep.
Who knows what adventures would happen tomorrow?

Welsh Vocabulary

Learn new words with Draig and Llygoden

dragon = draig

mouse = llygoden

tree = coeden

thunder = taran

nose = trwyn

fire = tân

sun = haul

 moon = lleuad

 stars = sêr

 book = llyfr

A series of original Welsh books for children – produced and published in Wales. All books in the series include a new English translation of the text.

Already published:

1. Morus yr Ystlum
Sheelagh Thomas-Christensen
0 86243 396 7

2. Gloria a'r Berllan Bupur
David Greenslade
0 86243 415 7

3. Dewi'r Llyfrbryf
Wayne Denfhy
0 86243 391 6

4. Peiriant y Tywydd
Catrin Evans
0 86243 412 2

5. Iona'r Iâr
Dylan Thomas
0 86243 434

6. Deio a'i Drwmped
Leon Balen
0 86243 463 7

7. Carwyn a'r Anrheg Nadolig
Mari Gwilym
0 86243 483 1

8. Arfon y Celt
Alan Rogers
0 86243 522 6

9. I Wlad yr Hwli Dwlis
Joan Ferrero
0 86243 560 9

10. Oli Olew
Catrin Evans
0 86243 573 0

11. Twinc, Cawr yr Ynys Binc
Fiona Wynn Hughes
0 86243 531 5

Also published in English:

Dai the Dragon-keeper
Alan Rogers
0 86243 562 5

**Wena and the
Weather Machine**
Catrin Evans
0 86243 561 7

Dragon and Mousie
Andrew Fusek Peters
0 86243 650 8

*For a full list of books currently in print, send now for your free copy
of our new, full-colour catalogue – or simply surf into our website at*
www.ylolfa.com